The Impossible Uprooting

David Waltner-Toews

poems

Canadian Cataloguing in Publication Data

Waltner-Toews, David, 1948-
The impossible uprooting

Poems.
ISBN 0-7710-8783-7

I. Title.

PS8595.A58156 1995 C811'.54 C94-932634-8
PR9199.3.W35156 1995

The publishers acknowledge the support of the Canada Council and the Ontario Arts Council for their publishing program.

Typesetting by M&S, Toronto
Printed and bound in Canada on acid-free paper

McClelland & Stewart Inc.
The Canadian Publishers
481 University Avenue
Toronto, Ontario
M5G 2E9

1 2 3 4 5 99 98 97 96 95

"... my life has been
a singing between the chance and the requirement."

–Pablo Neruda,
"Summary"

CONTENTS

HOW WE ARE PLUCKED

THE TIME OF OUR LIVES

for Kathy

I am having the time of my life
digging up an old pine stump
with my daughter
in the bright fall sunshine.
Everything I need to know about life
and death is in this moment.

The spade is singing
among the white-collared mushrooms:
Praise to the Fungi Imperfecti,
the Fusaria and the Cladospores.
The hatchet chops a tune
into the wood's soft heart:
Praise to the wood lice, the earthworms,
millipedes, hister beetles, common black
ground beetles, the slugs like ushers
waving their antennae at the calamitous lightspill.
Please close the door. The show's in progress.
Praise to the unseen saints of Gaia,
the Bacilli, the Clostridia,
and the pearly Micrococci.

Praise to the myriad of unseen
crawlies, the forgotten ones,
the bond breakers, hewers of cellulose
who make possible this uprooting.

After so many years
a friend becomes part of you.
Where the roots begin and the earth ends,

where pleasure, where pain,
where wishful memory, or truth,
cannot be dissected.
No point in spading here.
It is I myself who would be uprooted
if I uprooted you.

Time is an arrow
only in the briefest bug-life fragments,
and at the meteoric limits of our growth.
Where we live time is an inchworm,
rhythms of seasons and spades,
roots broken and re-sprung.
The stump is lifting
under the pry of my spade.
A mouth opens below,
a dark mouth singing
soft fleshy things,
singing multi-footed messengers,

singing a lieder of cycles –
the carbon cycle, the nitrogen cycle,
the water, the sulphur,
singing of the microscopic fixers,
singing lustily, with full synthesizer backup,
in chlorophyllic warbles,

who make me, Hominus Imperfecti,
possible, and you, and our sons
and our daughters, and
brightly, in the blue, sharp sunshine,
as the roots lift free, I am dug in,
rooted,
earthworms, beetles, fungi,

bacilli all around me,
skittling up the spade handle toward me, singing:

Welcome home.
Your turn is next.

LIFE ON THE VAGUS

A thought outleaps its purpose,
becomes a joey, slipping from its pouch,
the solitary thrill of sunwarmed hair
and a tango of conceptual
unbounding.

Our lives, replete
with vagaries
from brain to heart,
do not make sense,
yet reason lives
in every part.

For those who argue
that, since nature's all,
it's purposeless,
a thought is but a snake,
pure reason, the caged brain's
tongue articulating
spineless feet and crotches,
the un-imaginations
of death. Such thoughts
have all the wisdom of a pup
wagging in the snake's pursuit
who yelps when the quarry's tagged,
discovering his tail,
and licks amends.

So, for my part, let thoughts
outleap their pouch
slide vagus down from brain

in rhythm with the heart,
earth's beat, to being's watery ground,
like playing porpoises,
until once more in reason's air
they're found, like flying fish,
abounding.

POSTCARDS FROM JAVA: THE SUBTEXT

for Colin McLennan

i.

Mustafa swims naked
with the water buffaloes
slipping easily among the great
grey beasts. When the male
rears up to mount the female
his pink underbelly glistens.

Tomorrow from first light
well into the heat of the day
Mustafa's thin, muscular body
will slosh after the plough.
Then he will eat
his first bowl of rice.
Later, he will stoop along the roadways
cutting grass
to feed his buffaloes.

In the evening
they will bathe in the river.
I will drive by
and remark how beautiful.
I will take a picture for my album.

ii.

Little children in white shirts
and red shorts splash through monsoon puddles
after me.
Hello hello they call I love you.
Laughing, they have such
wonderful dark eyes, clean smiles,
such barefoot carefreeness.

In Jakarta when the rainy season
floods the open sewers
garbage and manure
spill into the houses of shanty towns.
Out of ten children
maybe six will survive.

iii.

The man on the bicycle
is carrying four chairs
and a table on his head.
Such a marvellous feat:
he should be in a circus.

All day in the market
he tries to sell his table
and chairs. In the evening
tired dirty hungry
he pedals his furniture home.

iv.

Agus fell from a coconut palm,
paralyzed him from the waist down.
They can grow shorter coconut trees.
You could almost pick the nuts
from your wheelchair with a stick,
like postcards from the hotel rack,
but they do not sway seductively,
nor conjure romance from a photograph.

v.

Tugiyah rides double
on her bicycle with Ninik.
Ninik, eight, wears a red skirt and white top.
Tugiyah, eleven, wears a blue skirt and white top.
They ride to school.
They speak Javanese.
They read Indonesian.
Their father speaks Javanese.
He reads the times changing
in his rice paddy.

Tugiyah's bike goes faster
if she clings to Mulyoko,
who has a motorbike.
They wobble speedily among the crowd
of vehicles on the road.
At one corner they wobble too much
and fall over.
The oil truck cannot swerve in time.
The becak driver cannot pedal fast enough.

The hospital is missing some equipment.
There is too much blood, and there is not enough.

Their friends can read about it in the newspaper
after the news about the drop in oil prices.
Their father looks at the paddy.
A good crop this year,
maybe enough to buy Ninik
her own bicycle.
But who will help gather the harvest?

THE HUNT

for Bert Lobe

The peasants for some paisa
beat the bushes,
hewing, crying in a mob
toward our deadly welcome:
three shotguns and a camera.

They flush
the wild boar,
dry branches snapping.
The hairy black thing breaks free
of the underbrush, breaks
his stride, his tusks
unbroken. The spirit of the bracken
comes for us.

I'm capturing
this dying moment's fuss
on film, straight
for the lens his rush,
like an American:
NOT ME, I'M PRESS! REALITY EXEMPT!

He's dropped just short
of thrusting by a burst of gunfire.

At the bonfire feast
I stand apart,
in back-brain's dark developing
this image:

a chunk of meat, fire-crisped,
hair and bone splinters catching in my teeth,
a small spray of sparks
fizzling in the drunken night

and from the woods around,
deep, stifling fear.

Bihar, India

BREAKING FREE THE WHALES
(On Loving Earth Not Wisely, But Too Well)

In a kind of wild exuberance

caught perhaps from the wet lash
of arctic wind
or the icy slap of brine
against our thighs
or the glimpse of bright sun glinting
from their hulls, we threw ourselves
into the thick of it,
the thick ice crust
creaking, bending under
the sheer weight of our dancing.

No rewards could supplant
our surge into the swell of open sea,
no cracks in our seeming solid prow,
no listing to starboard,
no regrets. Even knowing we've polluted
good intentions with these giant fantasies,
confusing poor navigational genes
with nature's pure desires,
nothing can overpower

this sense: the dry-lipped tropic heat
of too much loving,
however ill-conceived,

this sight: their gentle laugh
like a spout like a flag unfurled,

like a hand waving
as they crest a distant wave,

while under us
the ice crackles.

SIMULATION III

for JM

The researcher's a juggler,
a jester in the world's blind light
amid cacophonies of peers.
In paradigms like tents, dark with publication,
the world throws me
things: dead animals, bacteria,
farmers, leadened opinions,
parasite eggs in fecal flotations.
It is my job to find their high-flown
meaning in the computer's virtual space.

It makes no sense.
My back aches;
my eyes sting with sweat.
My brain balks at this world in fragments,
thought-borne data-points
like a million knives
a-glitter in the dome.
A Chicken Little juggler,
I fear the patternless
crash,
despair.

Then, in one flashed spray
of right relationships,
like playful divers
hung from the sky, the knives lock hands
in sweet array, so logical, a perfect fit.
Enthralled, I bow, take credit, publish.

Committees in the dark applaud,
nod, give tenure.

The moment tumbles.
The flash of intuition's light turned down,
the pattern is opaque:
in the computer, an infection's seasonal peak;
in the pasture, a dead foal, an angry farmer,
road apples steaming in the sun.
A mare, for no apparent reason,
kicks up her heels and gallops.

SURGERY

She's not been eating well, the cow.
Nothing that a cut can't cure.
Slit down through leather, yellow fat,
the muscles' lips come puckering,
beslobbering your rubber gloves with secrets,
things nature meant no one to see.
Seeing beyond what nature meant will
earn your fee. Now then, my dear,
stand quietly. Tell all.

She slams her foot up,
a bovine exclamation: I'm tender there!
She wants to render secrets
only to a grassy mound.
Her secrets, you cuttingly respond,
may speed her to the renderer.
This hits a raw nerve.
The scalpel stabs your wrist
as the hoof wallops your elbow.
This, you tell yourself, is good:
she's turning out her anger
from anorexic suicide
to murder. She'll live.
You wrap your wrist, keep cutting.
She'll tell you more
before the session's over.

Inside, she's steamy, warm.
You revel in erotic passages,
life's slippery mysteries.
It all feels normal,

like freshly boiled pasta.
Feels kinda twisted up,
you tell the farmer.
I'll just re-arrange a bit.
Re-frame the pain: it's a challenge,
not an obstacle. Folly suffered
is wisdom gained.

The cow stands quietly
as you stitch up,
neat cross patterns,
like her life – like all our lives,
in retrospect.

Later, she is eating well,
production up. You take credit,
or at least money.
Your healing touch
starts here: the airing of dark secrets,
not so much dark as deep, all muscle
and blood, really,
long-term grievances adhering to mucosa.

Still, she's tender there,
along the flank, you at your wrist.
A passing comment
at a party brings a twinge,
a cow's hoof in the gut,
sweet memories on ice,
a bitter, faintly comic twist.

Not a bad way to make a living:
verse by scalpeled verse,
and stitch by tugging,

pain-remembering stitch.
Never complete, this sort of cure,
this secret-giving,
it's much like poetry: the pain recurs,
and healing's pleasurable itch.

THE ECOLOGY OF POETRY

for Rod, Lorna, Katherine, Lisa, and Tanya

If tomorrow is at the door
and today, dishevelled on the couch,
still hasn't had her coffee,
don't let him in. Tomorrow can ruin today.
He'll drag out the better part of your day,
the pink skirt maybe,
and worry ragged holes into it
like a nesting hamster.
Do you need that?

Yesterday is bad enough,
and last week sprawled on the guest bed
and a few years ago scattered
about like floor cushions. Party guests
who stayed the night, they have bad breath and hangovers.
Like leftovers, plates of them, rotting around me.

We should all have compost heaps
spaded deep into our souls,
with modest wooden covers. Honey,
could you empty the can under the sink?
It's smelling ripe already –
bits of pain, scraps of ecstasy,
moments full of people, love, regret,
wine and maudlin verse.

The days of throwing out are over.
The world's already littered with our junk –
personal anger, revenge, passions made over
into public illusions of righteousness:

submarines named Corpus Christi and all those phallic
missiles. But if you just keep them in
you'll rot along with them, a confused heap
of smelly memories. The neighbours will complain.

The compost heap is singing.
If I don't sing along it will drive me insane.
If I sing, the neighbours will know I already am.
So I already am. I cannot help myself,
singing. I am eating my own leftovers,
ludicrously, tragically, as if I enjoy them.
I do enjoy them.

That is why I am here, near midnight,
kneading this lump of doughy past.
Tomorrow morning, fresh biscuits.
Oblivious to the future's wry shadow
slipping in, a cold gust tailing
the complaining cat, I'll go out.
All the way to the office, whistling.

All the old familiar notes.
A whole new song.

THE IMPOSSIBLE UPROOTING
(A Canadian Elegy)

for Jim and Marg at their 25th wedding anniversary

"There ain't no cure for love."
– Leonard Cohen

Imagine this – someone you love,
out of the blue, becomes a cripple,
a love-challenged person. Imagine love without arms,
hugless, or skinless, say, like loving
your grandmother's bone china –
awfully pretty that – Don't touch!
or worse yet thoughtless love, sans fantasies,
like loving the vacuum cleaner,
brainlessly nosing into the cushions.
Or imagine that your friend
is of a sudden gone, and you are left
hugging the vacuum itself, without even the comfort
of a machine or a body,
say your father dies, or your sister,
or the country you call home.

When you imagine this
you discover the full depth of your love.
You will find that love is a potted plant
with roots all through you.
You may want to match your loved one
cut for cut, to be like them –
except maybe not dead –
so you snip off just a bit,
one side of your tongue perhaps,
the mirror image of your love,
so you can be symmetrical,

his and hers handicaps, a broken person
in a broken country.
The aches ooze out.
The heart recoils in pain.
Or you think you can uproot a part,
just one small part, a slight perhaps,
something to do with flags or a dress she wore,
the memory of a song, or flowers in the streets, or tanks,
and the pain tingles like a million tiny knives
through every nervelet of your body
even as you tug gently, gently.
There is no escape from this:

The people you love
are stuck into you forever.
They grow with you.
They are what hold you together.

If you love someone
there is no end to it,
no future, in the fullness of enmity,
but to let go, succumbing to love's composting
rejuvenation, a heap of singing,
anger, hockey games, broomball on ice,
wild poetry, hot chili, a kitten hit by a car
and buried by the lilac bush,
rooting out into the whole garden
into the whole earth, until,
before you know it, the whole thing,
the whole confounded rootbound globe,
is caught by your love.

There you are, rooted, blooming,
a-tangle with borders, mother-tongues, sovereignty,

essential national interests, history's lead earrings,
her poisonous perfume, revenge masking as justice,
all that slimy, fuzzy-headed stuff in the refrigerator
for which the world, finally,
has lost its stomach, heart, brain,
rotting in and around you,
until God herself, garden-gloved,
spade in hand, steps out through some black hole,
heaven's gate, flicks back her hair
from a radiant, sweaty face.
She's on the prowl for something of a centrepiece
to grace the table at the time's-end feast.
Her gaze like butterflies alights on you,
your eyes surprised like summer daisies,
afraid that the season is over,
that you will now be judged, in the middle of this big messy
free-for-all, just-for-all, half-angry tangle,
where the sweet smell of your loved one's
underarm bacteria makes you feel suddenly at home,

and you discover in your shock how we are plucked
by our own fearless letting go, judged in the solar system's
final super-nova laugh not by how safely we have hoarded and
preserved, not by ideas in the bank or seeds kept dormant, cold,
but by the velvet curve and colour of the petals
in the dim light we unfold.

A WORD IN THE NEST

A WORD IN THE NEST

Rummaging through an old trunk in the attic
I pull out yellowed, crinkled pictures:
my five-year-old mother with a cow,
my four-year-old father on a horse,
the long, warm day before the Revolution,
forever summer, forever Sunday,
forever seen through the sepia of suffering,
the uncle dragged by the hair
and skewered by Ukrainian anarchists
with raging hair and laughter like gunfire.
What did it mean, that rough hand upon my parents,
dragging them by the scruff to this God-forsaken promised land?
What is wrong with these pictures –
my brother, hair untrammelled,
expounding alternative lectures at Harvard, 1968;
my little sister, hair cut smartly,
in a once-forbidden, twice-bold cap and gown, 1974;
me, forever sitting on a hard bench, my hair slicked back,
half-listening through a veil of humid Sundays,
folding church bulletins into boats?

Unexpectedly, the sun slants through a hole
where the fat black squirrel has broken through,
and, settling through the dust, alights
on a thought, a small, hard thought, like a crown tucked away
from the Sunday School Christmas program.
It sparkles with history and irony,
circled with haloes.

This is my heirloom, my crown in glory,
the jewels I have pilfered from the homeless

in the golden streets. This is my country,
the place we landed, children of the ones who fled,
carrying, in our leaky, near-sinking minds,
the ones they left behind, gaunt and righteous ghosts
who haunt us. And the others, now, the ancestors
we inherit, parents of this orphaned multi-country,
tugging at my sleeve in the grimy press
of the street's hot current,
the Bihari mother with the pleading eyes
and the blank-eyed babe-in-arms,
in the senseless bite of chilled fall air,
the kids, those other Indians, sniffing gasoline
behind a tin shack,
the kids with one arm, beggars with one leg,
something cut off
to enhance photogenicity,
an eye plucked, the piercing harp of poverty,
the tens of thousands every year
shrinking back from their bodies,
from life, the little temples
where the flies congregate,
the choking veil of dust
where the words gather, swirl up
into the hot blue,
the slow vultures circling

almost a poem.

Our jewels are the currency
of righteousness; they are how we recognize
each other on the street, the sparkle in our teeth,
the secret wink of TV preachers, presidents, prime ministers,
chief executive officers.

They are the force in so much writing
I admire, the best of my generation, the better half,
the victims, the survivors,
makers of rocks in snowballs,
Suzanne on a white horse
screaming, scattering diamonds
and splatters of blood, the betrayed,
the young girl dragged by the hair
and skewered by avuncular self-righteousness,
the justice of her cause
the rat-at-at of laughter shriek of pain
driving her to battle, in the sleet of conventional wisdom
up the slippery rock face
of power, parliament the senate the premier's house,
to plant her flag.

I am left with the rabble in her wake.
I cannot claim that suffering.
I stand accused: white, male, middle class,
neither Margaret Atwood, nor Leonard Cohen,
not even part Indian, maybe even part German.
The fat red-faced digit rising insufferably
from my groin accuses me
erect with self-intoxication,
pleasing tautly even as it mocks.
I have no claim on righteousness.

But listen: I am sick of all this,
sick of the insufferable claims of ancestors,
the sins of parents binding us to bitterness.
There is no just claim on righteousness,
neither by Mennonites nor Muslims nor Jews nor Palestinians
nor conservatives nor socialists nor Real Women nor Real Men
nor Robert Bly nor Gloria Steinem nor the poor nor the Blacks

nor the rich nor the Irish nor the Americans
nor the Québécois nor the cowboys nor the descendants
of displaced noblemen nor murdered serfs nor crucified children.
Neither by the pious nor the powerful nor the sceptical.
Neither by you nor by me.
There is no righteousness in suffering.
There is no poetry in it.
There are no words but the vultures,
the last words, unspoken.
Words are no currency for suffering or righteousness.
There is only the brutal claw that snatched my bread
on the Benares railway platform,
lifting away before even the shock could register.

When it is gone,
my sandwich,
the suffering I have seen
or heard or read about,
the little samosas of my pretence, gone,
I am left clutching at air,
clawing at something more humble,
a frail small nest of bones and flesh,
a body no better than Hitler's,
myself, yourself.

There are many ways to see us.
We can look elsewhere; there are mirrors
all around: let us begin with the Old Country.

My grandmother, survivor
of famines and revolutionary omelettes,
home from her tempting in the white and futuristic hospital
(A desert, she confided, truly, the hospital is a desert)
stretched out her hand

past the clean-frocked doctor, as Moses above the dry rock,
staring at the space over his shoulder
almost tempting him, even, to look
where he could not believe.
Ja, I am coming, she said,
and in the embarrassed silence
the clear callop callop
of horses up a gold-cobbled street,
that once-and-future place,
and the peace of her face against the pillow.
And all around the shells
the pretty shells
exploding.

Here is another image in the glass, our side,
the side we fled to from the Old Country,
now in another's
promised land, coming home
to ourselves.
I read about us in the newspaper
saving democracy in El Salvador.
We threw a baby
into the air, her mother watching.
We caught her
with our bayonets.

We worry about coffee and cholesterol.
We eat and drink from worry.
After the evening TV news
we set our heads down,
empty cups on the counter.

How we dabble at faith!
We sing about Golgotha,

our voices a pillow to conscience,
our grand collections
never more than thirty pieces.

I am a mother,
my child laughing in the air,
the child, Christ
have mercy on us.

It is also possible to simulate this:
a country, a place, a future.

Trailing our rags like
academic credentials,
we stumble numb-footed
through the pining forest
gathering data,
fragments of half-rotten logs,
the debris of mid-winter's
chattering interview
with trees.

Bent over, bark-laden
we return, stomp our feet
free of snow
and stack the data bit by bit
into a hearth-side file.
Then, rubbing our hands
in cold anticipation,
we enter our hard-won knowledge
into the computer.

Chunk by number-crunching chunk
it burns; our brains

feel warmed.
We shall be well-informed.
At the end of a long evening
we will be poking
through a small pile of ash.
This is the essence of the forest.
This is the suffering of trees, quantified.
This is what will not be left
for the children.
We will know how many gasps they have left.
It will be in the conclusions:
this is what our country is really like,
what it will become.
We are ready to write our research report.

It will be in the final couplet.
I am ready to write my poem.
There is no difference.
Outside, the wind is howling
and the trees cackle.

Listen: is that the ocean in this shell?
Are you shelling peas?
Is this the fall?
Are they shelling Sarajevo?
Is this mortal shell exploding?
Do we all fail to gather?
Shall we all fall together?

There are too many babies in the world
and not enough vegetables.
Paul Ehrlich says so. And the World Bank.
I have seen the thin-limbed balloons
stunned beyond outcry.

They are dry, pulpy vegetables
suitable for serving tyrants.

There are too many vegetables in the world
and not enough children,
too many babies stolen at night,
pilfered by scarecrows
dragged like onionskins on string
into a desert without end
to serve the tyrants,
wealth and power, to serve us,
who feed our bodies and our compassion
on the harvest of their undoing,
our currency shrivelled
like last year's carrots.

Oh lovers, pray for rain.
Plant succulent tomatoes.
Sow grass on hillsides.
Lead kids among the children among the trees.
Give the babies milk and honeysuckle,
blankets, sanitary bathrooms, a glass of water.
Unsettle the tyrants with your crowing,
betray them with a cock,
stuff their mouths with straw.

This is the rain dance,
the end of all reigns,
a dance for children
and fresh baby carrots,
a little two-step
when no one is looking.

Every good beginning
is just this small.

And one bad ending,
the end we justify,
looks like this:
the squirrel smacked
in Washington DC rush-hour traffic
as it streaks between the cars
suddenly, stunned on its back, legs twitching
in disbelief. I see it two cars ahead
fling itself to its feet
barely start, smacked again,
flung from tire to tire,
steel to steel.
In the haziness of my rear-view mirror
he disappears.

This is the sacrifice;
we pray in our four-wheeled cubicles
before the stolen fire,
the fire from ages past, the green ages;
this is the god for whom we kill
in the hot sand,
the choking sacrifice of children.
This is our way of life,
the cost.

Tell me of your righteousness.
I'll tell you of mine.

We were good Mennonite boys.
We smoked toilet paper in the bathroom
at school. We joked about big mammaries and miniskirts.

We played pocket pool. We had boners.
We avoided thinking about whether our fathers had them,
and how they kept them from showing, impossibly,
with Bibles or loose change.
We thought about what we were warned against
and whether it might be fun, or just dangerous.
We wondered about the unforgivable sin.
We looked for secret messages from God
in random Bible flips.
We all got into the car and drove down to the pool hall.
We wondered if this meant we were on the road
to hell. We learned how to play.
We knew we were lost.

Some of us got married,
loved in that sweet lawless distillation
of lust friendship commitment.
We cried
not because we were sensitive guys,
just because, sometimes, we couldn't stand it.
We cooked and washed dishes.
This wasn't some kind of penance,
the burden of a faultless guilt,
some kind of badge.
This just was; we wanted to live here, too.
Some of us worried too much,
laughed about it,
went on, undecided,
had kids anyway.

This is where we get back to the kids.
When I think about them
I am in an empty room smelling of old wood
and mustiness. The window is open to a cool dusk.

I can hear the bees
swarming. They will settle like a thousand
soft painful flowers
covering my body.
They will swarm inside my skull
buzzing softly.
These are the thoughts
of my children.

unless nations sail the way of bell bottoms
        the bell tolling one last time
unless we wring out every last bit of sense
unless we are not for sale
unless this is the bottom line
unless the toll is finally too high
unless the tree cutters the plastic clutterers
        the money terrorists the cultists of competition
        can see their feet the clay well-heeled concede defeat
unless our crews dismantle nuclear weapons
unless we create compelling reasons for them not to exist
unless we have compelling reasons to exist
unless there is enough rain
unless we can get by on less
unless we buy less
unless we use condoms don't smoke drink coffee
unless this doesn't matter
        (what does: do you love me?)
unless the ozone is whole again
unless the salmon spawn beyond our wiliest expectations
unless Gaia forgives
unless death has her dominion
unless her dominion is conditional
unless the politics of termites budworms cows potatoes
        seals cod whales and paycheques are one

unless the battles are won
unless the battles are only in our heads
unless the monkeys in Amazonia swing
unless the peasants in Amazonia eat
unless the monkeys of politics evolve
unless the grass grows greener
unless the other side is our side
unless we are fed
unless we are fed up with excess
unless we all have a stake in this
unless feedlots carlots stockyards stockmarkets
    lotteries of life and ozone death are undone
unless we are not proud
unless we pride ourselves on kindness
unless we admit a mistake sometimes
    about God capital punishment the right amount of nutmeg
unless you can, simply, accept your belle bottom
    my love for it
unless I mop the kitchen floor, singing
unless we plant the hyacinth bulbs before first frost
unless this is not a crock-and-bull story
unless this is not a china shop
unless we all shop in China
unless one quarter of us eat are happy have enough
unless enough is enough
unless angels peace mercy flower from the bulbs of blood below
    Los Angeles Kabul Tienanmen Square Santiago Prague Sarajevo
unless we are appalled by the sight of blood
unless we are the blood of Gaia
unless we are neutrophils geophils had our fills
unless Marta Kumsa walks talks lives free
unless Nelson Mandela Stephen Biko Lee Tae-Bok
    Mykola Korbal Jack Mapanje Bethony Pierre-Paul
    Rebecca Tulalian Ana Maria Martinez Abdulla Basturk

        Wong Souk Yee Chng Suan Tze Taysir Aruri Chen Erjin
        and all their children friends lovers enemies are invited
        sit down partake in a Jewish-Mennonite-Italian-Arab feast
        singing eating laughing
unless the wounds heal
unless we can live with the scars
unless we are in good humour
unless this is out of our hands
unless we put our hands our arms down
unless you are in my hands I in yours
unless there is a child who remembers
        cares   can write
unless puffers and wrasse delight the coral
unless our wrath is wrapped in chorales
unless we sing in four parts
unless we think in three parts
        left right corpus callosum
unless we are not driven to despair
unless we are not driven
unless we bicycle
unless we walk in the crisp fall sunshine
        full pale October moon   God's pretty joke
unless everything is in its season
        apples fall pumpkin pie rightly seasoned
unless we love us
unless we talk about it before and after words
unless there is no word for it
unless it does not dominate us
unless we accept death
unless we celebrate babies
unless we have fewer of them
unless we have fewer of us
unless the babies of Sudan Somalia Chad Ethiopia
        can run laugh read sing

unless we play duets with them
    dance calypso eat dhal-puri buss-up-shut
    curried chicken borscht cabbage rolls rollkuchen
    real fat dripping sugar digging at your teeth
    food with consequences
unless the earth is food for thought
unless we have food in our bellies
unless spirit is the music body is the horn
    spirit is the chicken body is the barn
    body is the accident spirit saves from harm
unless we trombone slide me in you
unless we are not in limbo
unless we limbo
    singing under the lowest bar
    ears tuned to the earth   knees to heaven
unless justice is just this enough
unless we get over the lost several billion tears
unless we share our parochial soup primordial stew
unless we sin sing symbiotically
    forgiving even as we are
unless we are for giving
unless this is a given
unless we love us
    it is not sublime
    it is useless
    it is sublimation
    it is pointless
    we will be roundly defeated
unless we have the nerve to live in the vagus
    in the vagaries between brain and heart
there is nothing to say.

There is nothing to say.

In the cooking the spices the wine the laughter our bodies
in the sighing of the compost, turning
in the slap and song of the floor and mop
in the lingering care of children
in what we have forgiven
in how we ride the rushed hours' vagaries
in the comfort we have given
in the silence which rings
in how, like children in the sun's last glare
like small, frail nests
we raise our hands to the wings
the wings descending

we have said everything.

MENNONITE BLUES

THE GIFT

for Mother, who has survived revolution, civil war, drought, famine, being orphaned, emigration, servant work, motherhood, widowhood, and much more, on her 75th birthday

After the first sharp cry
it is not a question, this life,
of what has been survived.
It is what has survived.

It is not your father gone,
swarthy faces at the window with guns.
In the kitchen, it is Mother's hum,
a cup of fresh warm milk, and a bun.

It is not Mother reduced to the bone's
terrible whisper, nor a house abandoned.
It is the train like a bright snake amid the ruins,
a bird soaring, crying, in its flight home.

It is not the hopelessness of loss,
rude officials at greasy shipyards, and dust.
It is a young woman from overseas, the kindness in her face,
setting out the doctor's tea in blue china cups.

Of that new land as flat as plautdietsch
where even the zwieback loomed significant,
and pluma moos for all the Englisch knew
was some kind of deer to shoot

and a horse a husband five bushy-haired
kids a house – several houses, one finally with no steep stairs –

a real freezer for meat buns and cookies and a recreation room
to hide the television, we can really only claim

the cookies, which we did, still frozen,
as our first tangible recollection.
But even this – our remembering and remembering of
remembrance –
will pass, and our children's.

It is not the quartz-sharp grit deeply clasped
by the heart which we inherit, nor the pain's lingering grasp.
It is you, here, now, the rich, opaquely buffed layers
of your life, like a pearl before us.

ERIC REIMER, FROM

In 1913, when Eric Reimer
was a child in the Ukraine,
his family was from East Prussia.
In 1920, as a young boy in Winnipeg,
he was from the Ukraine,
though the family name,
his father explained,
could be traced back to Germany.
About 1939, it was discovered
that the family lineage
actually went back to Holland,
and that the German period was short,
if not non-existent.
In the early 1940s, intensive perusal
of family documents
suggested the possibility of some Russian blood,
but by 1946 this was clearly demonstrated
to be mere wild conjecture.
During a brief period
while crossing the border
on the way to go shopping in Minneapolis,
Eric Reimer was born "east of Ottawa."
He later admitted this to be inaccurate,
however; his mother bore him
somewhere in West Germany
while escaping from the Russians.
In 1965, Eric retired to Abbotsford, B.C.,
where he was from Winnipeg, Manitoba.
He died just two years later
in the Clearbrook shopping centre,
where he was from the Menno Home For The Aged.

After a moment of being
neither here nor there
Eric Reimer appeared in heaven.
There he met God, from Everlasting,
who looked up from the book He was reading
and said, Well then, Eric Reimer,
where are you going?

ROOTS

not about Rudy Wiebe, but for him

Rudy Wiebe, wiping the sweat from his brow,
calls a spade a spade.
He has a spade in his hands.
He is digging a hole near Winnipeg
in the middle of a potato field.
He has blisters on his hands.
He has roots on the brain.
He is looking for his roots.
One foot down he unearths
a nest of potatoes.
Two feet later he has an aching soul
and a sore foot.

His spade has struck a bone.
It is a dry bone.
It gets up and walks around.
Rudy is not sure if it is an ankle bone
or a hip bone.
It may be the bone of a buffalo
dropped by an Indian's arrow or of an Indian
killed by Mennonite good fortune.
Perhaps a Mennonite died here
of overwork and too many potatoes.
Most likely it is the bone of a cow
that choked on a potato.
Rudy Wiebe cannot tell for sure
what kind of bone it is.
He watches the bone walk out to the road
and head toward town.

The people in Winnipeg ignore the bone.
To them, it is just another drunk Indian.

After the bone
Rudy Wiebe takes a lunch break.
He sits beside the hole and eats
rollkuchen with watermelon.
After lunch he continues his search.
There is a lot of dirt in the hole.
There is a lot of dirt in Winnipeg.
The bone gets tired of Winnipeg
and comes back out to the field.
It sits on the nest of potatoes
and watches the top of Rudy's head
going up and down in the hole
between sprays of dirt.

By nightfall Rudy Wiebe
is up to his ears in dirt
but he still hasn't found any roots.
He tilts back his hard hat
shoulders the spade
and trudges home,
bone in hand.
How was your day? asks his mother.
No luck, he says
hanging up his hat.
Maybe you are right.
Maybe my roots are in Russia.

My my, says his mother.
You have enough dirt behind your ears
to grow potatoes.
Rudy pulls a nest of potatoes

out from behind his ear.
Rudy and his widowed mother are very poor.
For supper they have potato soup
with a bone in it.
When I was a girl in Russia,
says Rudy's mother,
we ate this all the time.

WINNIPEG

for Hildi, a fellow refugee

"Then if any man say unto you, Lo, here is Christ, or there, believe it not."

– Matthew 24:23

The night we had wave
after crashing wave of thunder
bouldering down the clouds
I could almost imagine Winnipeg again,
God come down in Edmonton or Toronto
or some other God-forsaken place,
and Winnipeg, she there on her knees
rinsing her soiled hair
in the Red, the Assiniboine snaking
at her skirts, she so cursing angry,
shrieking plautdietsch at Portage and Main:

To have come so far
halfway around the world
and still to have missed the Chosen Place
it must not be!

The Real Messiah will come singing
Handel to Winnipeg, reeking of borscht
and rollkuchen, porzeltche and paska,
round as a laughing Buddha
but not laughing, serious like raw cabbage
or an uprooted potato, but not so offensively poor,
a washed potato perhaps, singing
certainly, a baritone, a fine baritone,
good enough for Hymn Sing,
and after him a whole cherubic chorus

singing kernlieder
singing the Hallelujah Chorus
singing, for a grand finale,
just before the food,
Praise God From Whom All Blessings Flow.

And here in this smug country
in the middle of a summer storm
I could almost imagine the Aryan devil
come down in Winnipeg, singing Wagner,
the clashes here but faint reverberations
of that mad embrace
the ecstasy of fierce frustration.
See God what you have missed!
the love-hate scream thundering
from see to churchly see.

And I could almost imagine us
sitting with Jesus, a lean and barely laughing
loin-clothed raconteur, in Edmonton or Toronto,
drinking wine from bowls filled
from the washroom tap, feeling just a little
sentimental, drawing circles
with our fingers on the table,
waiting
for another parable
waiting
for the storm to pass over,
looking up to see Him gone
and in the distance, from Winnipeg perhaps,
the exquisite consummation:
Bach's Magnificat
in Low German.

TANTE TINA'S LAMENT

Haenschen is a fool
and I am his mother,
Dear Lord, forgive us both.
Haenschen in the city
struts, like a chicken.
He is wearing a pink shirt
and plaid, big-bottomed hosen.
When he was little,
his bottom was like a zwieback.
His little buns I spanked
and how he crowed!

Now his tongue he wags at me
and thinks I am ignorant.
He says farmers have no brains,
they should all be businessmen.
He says farm girls don't know how to walk
and I a steak don't know how to barbecue.
Oh his heart is full of borscht,
and his words are like sour cream.
Don't called me Haenschen, he says.
My name is John.
Do I not know my son's name?
Did I not for six nights with my man Doft
about that name argue already yet?

On Wednesday night
the young people go to church.
They are platz eating and testimonies giving.
The girls have long golden hair.

Their cheeks are rosy from harvest
and dresses their knees cover.
When the young people together sing
it is heaven above and earth below
with sopranos and basses.

But my Haenschen
to the city goes, to dance.
He has a girl friend.
On her lips she has red grease gesmeared.
Her blond hair is cut and curled
and her knees are bare
like a young calf.
When they are dancing
their legs are noodles
and the music is a tractor.
The girl friend says it is not a shame
a woman her hair to be cutting.
She thinks Mennonites are like Hutterites
and has never heard of rollkuchen.
What good can come of that?

Haenschen says she is a modern girl.
He says we must speak Englisch to her
because she to the United Church goes.
He says Low German is a pile of manure.
Listen here, my little boy.
I will surround you with Low German.
I will piles of it to you be speaking.
Then you will know what Low German is!
Then you will remember
a mother's anger is a willow switch.

He does not listen.
We are poor, he says.
We do not know how people are money making.
He wants to be rich, like the Englische,
and from mannagruetze to save us all.
His heart is tight as a pfeffernuss.
His head is a piroshki
with fruit stuffed.

In the barn, the cats eat mice
and for milking time they are waiting.
When my man comes in
I serve him dinner on a china plate.
But my son does not know happiness.

On New Year's Eve
we go to church at night,
and on Easter
when the sun rises
we are singing praises.
Haenschen is at church by eleven
on Easter.
On New Year's Eve
he goes dancing.
He is not even coming the children to hear
on Christmas Eve.
When he was still a bursch
he was a wise man in the play.

Oh my son
my heart so heavy is
thick as glums.
If you come home
it will rise, light and sweet.

I will make you porzeltche for breakfast
and every morning the New Year
we will celebrate.

TANTE TINA TALKS ABOUT HER MAN

He was a schlingel, my man Doft,
since long already
before I had him,
but this he later forgot.
We came once over to dinner
at their house at the Namaka farm
all aufgedressed from church,
close around the table,
the steak in sauce so good
from in the oven all through church baking
you could eat it with a spoon,
and potatoes mashed with a loch
in the middle for gravy.
We were all smelling so much
we could hardly hold ourselves for eating
and Mr. Reimer he little Doft asks to pray
with his brother Pete.
We are all thinking they will say
"Segne Vater diese Speise
Uns zur Kraft and Dir zum Preise Amen"
but together they sing
"Eetle ottle black bottle
Eetle ottle out Amen"
and then burst out laughing like horses
blowing through the nose.
Mr. Reimer was so angry
he said nothing
but the boys dragged by the neck
out to the barn
so we the cries couldn't hear.
And even after Mrs. Reimer prayed

Elsie and I were still ashamed
for being children and thinking the boys
did it for us, to show off, ja,
so we into our plates looked
and haven't much eaten.

But Doft he was never one for learning.
There was the time an Englische preacher
from the city came and spoke
about tithes and offerings
for the konferenz, and Doft has his tie
into the collection plate put. And already
once he in Bible School was
Bob Friesen from Winnipeg came to visit
to the farm and Doft let him ride
the one horse who loved the barn
more than anything,
so when they went out it was slow
like going to the front to get saved,
but coming back
it was fast like a pig running
and when they through the door of the barn
back galloped his knees
scraping clean the skin off
the Friesen boy his pants filled,
and Doft was in the straw laughing.

We have ourselves found
in Bible School and have been married
when the dust storms were thick in the air
and the wind like a choir of chicken manure
from the coulee was singing.
My white dress and Doft's navy suit and our faces
all were grey

so in the pictures
we already old looked yet.

The more hard we worked
the more the Lord blessed
the more pious was my man
until how many were the cows
and how big was the tractor
and the word of the Lord
all were the same.

The two girls came
and could zucker platz make
but my man had no platz except for Haenschen
who came after,
and then only in the barn.
Haenschen, he was just like his father
and that last time he Doft to the barn called,
Come quick to see!
so he through the door went
and down the milk pail on his head
is spilling –
after the wide pants and the dancing
that was the last thing.
Doft so hard hit him with the stick
until the blood came
and after Haenschen for sure
nothing of the farm wanted
and in his fancy hosen to the city went
and from church ist abgefallen.
My man is sitting then on the milk stool
and nothing saying.
Was ist zu sagen?

Then there came only work,
and no blessing.
Only once was he hitting me
when I something said,
but after he just stayed
from the house.

And then came the stroke.
I had to take him to the bathroom
and from the bed uplifting
and every day the Bible reading.
Always he to the wall looked only.
He had no tongue.
Once Haenschen came back
and by the bed stood
but the two schlingels
never a word spoke,
like two old pfeffernusse
to crack your teeth on
sitting after Christmas alone
on a kitchen plate.
It is past the time for eating
and they sit there only
remembering for you
that here the family once was.

At the funeral around the open box with Doft
we have stood for the picture,
Haenschen and me and Frieda and Katie.
I am thinking
so bad it wasn't
I wouldn't it again do.

I want only once more at the piano

to be playing
and my man still with his hair
cut around like with a topf over the head
and his cheeks red from the wind
singing in tenor
"Ich weiss einen Strom, dessen herrliche Flut
fliesst wunderbar stille durchs Land."

Then my heart like a mad goose is uprising
snapping and hissing
and I have to sit down on the bench
so much hurt there is.
"Haenschen," I say, "Friedchen, Kaetchen,
there is no more comfort for me.
Ya, if you love me
if you do not want me to die,"
I am with my hand the goose in my breast
downbeating,
"there is nothing to do," I tell them,
"but to have grandchildren."

HAENSCHEN'S SUCCESS

(Poor Immigrant Makes Good)

"But alas for you who are rich!"
cried the old blue denims.
Having outgrown them
I stuck them into a paper bag
and took them to the Mennonite Relief Store.
The grey-haired clerk
crinkled them open like an old songbook.
"What have we here?" he sang.
I shrugged my shoulders.
An iron-on seat patch glared at me.
"You have had your time of happiness!"
it shouted.
"What was that?"
asked the old man, cupping his ear.
I headed for the door.
"Yes, I'm sure they'll bring someone
happiness," he said, checking the pockets.

Out on the street
my corduroys hugged me.
I thrust my palms into their pockets
and we held hams
all the way home.
That night, religiously,
I hung them like a prayer
in my closet.

The next day my bells and I
were out strolling and they whispered,
snugging up against my thigh,
"You know, a man that has

really ought to have more,
don't you think?"
Well, it's not every day a man's pants
give him that kind of freedom!
We swung into a store
and before you could say Steinbach
Manitoba's Automobile City
there was a whole choir of cords
humming in my closet.

Now, when I the door swing open
in the morning
it's like a Hallelujah Chorus in cotton
singing me out into the day.
"Praise the Lord!" shouts the chorus.
"Thank you that we are not blue.
Thank you for this free country
where a man above his jeans can rise."
Thus, every day, scripture and my thighs
are fulfilled and I respond, "Dear Lord,
my heart pants for thee.
Hallelujah. Amen."

HAENSCHEN'S COMPLAINT

I am a father
and Johnny is my fool
God help him.
He swaggers like an Indian
in striped coveralls
and heavy leather boots.
He shuffles like his feet are cast in bronze.
When he was just a tyke
he wore the finest shoes.
I've had *them* bronzed
and set above the fireplace.

His tongue is a hundred-dollar cheque
written on a one-dollar brain account.
He says businessmen have no heart,
they should all be farmers.
He says city girls are prissy
and don't know how to make yogurt.
His words to me are like yogurt,
sour and with his own goodness dripping.
Don't call me, he says, I'll call you.
How sweetly he used to call me Papa!
Now he thinks
his father is a lending agency –
interest free!

On Wednesday night
the young people meet at our house.
They drink Seven-Up and swim in the pool.
The girls keep their curls above the water.

They bat their eyelashes
and show off new ensembles.
Later, the boys bring out guitars
and Gospel choruses they sing,
bouncy and clean as newborn babies.

But my appleseed
goes traipsing off to barn dances.
He has a girl friend
who says hair spray is unnatural.
Her hair is long and straggly.
She wears bluejeans
with patches on the seat.
When they dance
they stomp their feet and whoop
like a bunch of farmers.
The girl friend thinks Mennonites
wear big black hats.
She says Hutterites are with it
and has never a Hymn Sing seen on TV.
What kind of bringing up did she have?

Johnny says she is a modern girl.
He says we should be kind to her
because she's from Toronto.
He says education is for fools.
He should know: all the way
through college I sent him already yet,
the little wise guy.
Behind a barn I should have taken him
and with a textbook thrashed.
Then he would know what education is!

His ears are full of wax.
We are too rich, he says.
We don't know how to live right.
He wants us to be poor, like the Indians,
and save us all from income tax.
His heart, at every inconvenience, bleeds.
His head is like my mother's steak –
too long in the gravy left.

On the patio
my English sheepdog chews a milkbone
and my wife reads
Future Shock.
But my son cannot find happiness.

On New Year's Eve
we have church people over
and on Easter
we donate chocolates
to the Sunday School.
Johnny has a protest march
on Easter morning.
On New Year's Eve
he dances with tree huggers.
He doesn't even come on Christmas Eve
to hear the kids!
When he still was wet behind the ears
he was a shepherd in the play.

Oh my boy
what do you know about the price of land?
the dirt-floored houses and potato soup
we struggled out of?
If you come home

I'll plant in the back lawn a garden.
Every weekend, you can be pulling thistles.
And I'll never once, God help me, mention money.

FRIEDA'S TURN

for Tante Truda (1905-1991)

We were said to be quite the fetching girls
growing up on the farm in Altona,
you know the sort, girls fetch me some
milk from the cooler, girls fetch the laundry
from downstairs. Of course we also could
feed the calves the chickens the pigs and the men
and bake platz for Young Peoples.
We were quite the girls.

But only our little brother Haenschen
actually had a name. Only he
could be a proper saint in the barn
or a villain in plaid bell bottoms in town
and then, after his cursed business successes
so obviously blessed by God, a saint again.

We were just "the girls."
Katie, she stayed behind, wore earrings
and, in summer, sleeveless dresses to church,
her pale seductive shoulders
the colour of lightly toasted marshmallows,
such sweetness an affront to the brethren.
Each of us have our ways
of being whole.

She flirted from behind the tool counter
at the Winkler hardware store,
married a Rempel boy,
had a baby in six months.

But I was the elder.
A more serious departing was called for.
Ernie Regier the doctor's boy
offered to make me pregnant
and tried once in his Dad's Ford.
It was a spiritual success . . .
that is, technically a failure.
Aside from sewing machines and milkers
I never was much at technique.
Mom and Dad might have been pleased
had I had the nerve to confess;
on the other hand, they would no doubt
have concentrated on the weakness of having tried
rather than the triumph of my failure.

There was college, of course,
the going to it a travesty of faith,
the content irrelevant.
And the crowning glory,
three years of volunteer work
in Mexico, in the sizzling heat
organizing sewing and reading classes
for abused Mennonite girls no younger than me,
no different, but with less to eat, less to lose,
bound, whether they left or stayed,
went to grade school or got pregnant.

Back in Winnipeg in the bitter cold teaching,
no man would have me. Three years of intimate working
with the Lord – I was hopelessly compromised.
A missionary for life.

Well, there was Jake, who tried,
sort of. Married me, planted me in a new house

at the end of a muddy furrow
in new suburbia, while he traipsed off
to conferences. Konferenz, says Mother.
It's like the barn. It's where a man belongs,
with the manure.

Mother came to visit every Saturday.
One blue-bright fall day
she came back from the market
with two brown paper bags,
set them on the counter,
one with onions, lilies of the field,
she called them. In China, says Mother,
they are stomach cancer preventing.
I heard on the CBC.
The other with tulips.
She spent all afternoon on her knees
in the dirt, planting.
There, she said, rubbing the dirt from her palms
like flour after bread making.
In spring, the mud will blossom, ja?

All that winter, I waited
as the snow, that soft, cold quilt,
love-smothered me, then receded
like lace slipping down
from earth's dark shoulders.
I waited for the rows of two-lipped
Dutch girls, prim and pretty as Mennonites
the dark yard to be redeeming.

One day I called,
eyeing through the streaked glass
the green tongues wagging at me

from the flowers' dark bed.
Mother, I said, you know those tulips
you planted? Ja.
They were onions.
Oh how we laughed.
What good borscht I now could make!
Such a healing in the steamy kitchen!

Frieda, she called across the city
into the phone.
Frieda, if you are in the yard onions having
then I have the whole winter borscht
been making with tulips.

That fall, I went back to university,
then medical school,
always in my mind that phone call
and how in the long silence
I sat by the phone
smiling to myself.
Mother, I said. Ja.
You know how once you said
you wanted a doctor to be?
Ja.
It's not too late, Mother.
You have the gift.
And in her laughter
how the silver chalice in my mind
was rising,
fragrant with borscht and tulips.

TANTE TINA'S CHRISTMAS

Me it's not
what they want.
It's my stories.

Tell us how it was,
they ask me, imagine
my boy Haenschen and his little Haenschen
not so long ago just a little knirps
but now already with an anhaengsel. These girls
don't like me to say it so,
like they are something hanging on, but with names like
Angela and Mary-Jean, what else can I think?
Such names aren't Mennonite, that's sure.
But I love them, ja, they're my Haenschens'.
What can I tell?
So is das Leben.

Christmas afternoon the boys still groan
from too much turkey and potatoes,
eat halvah and play knipsbrat,
and the kids go out down the riverbank
tobogganing.
It's the same, like it was.
And before that, even,
Weinachtsabend, after the children's program
at church – you know little Haenschen
read a scripture this year?
Even with his hair so long
they let him read, praise God – even then,
before the plates for each child
under the tree go, we all sing

"Welch ein Jubel, Welche Freude,"
so nothing new under the sun comes.
I get older only.

Now they want stories,
how I walked to school in snow,
they want Russlaenda stories
from Opa and Oma.
Once, I tell them, we didn't all think
we could save the world.
That the Lord's work was.
Now even the girls go to college,
and what is coming of that?
A world without porzeltche
is not worth saving, or zwieback at least,
or borscht and rollkuchen,
but what do they know of that?

Ja, well, one time the Machnovites, the bandits, ja,
they came to our house in the Molotschna.
Everyone they would kill, they said, but Mutti
had borscht in a big topf steaming
and the men when they must choose
between their guns and a spoon for the borscht,
every time the spoon wins.
The soldiers ate themselves full
and went away, so you see? The Lord provides.
Haenschen, he likes that story
but his anhaengsel is not so sure.

Then I tell them,
Well that was my weinachtswuensch,
where is yours, and Haenschen, you know,
living in that big house with an Englische frau

he can still say:
"Da war einmal ein Mann
Er hatte eine Pfann
Die Pfann war ihm zu heiss
So ging er auf das Eis," und so weiter,
so I am happy.
And little Haenschen the grandboy with the hair
he can sing with the guitar:
"Haenschen klein ging allein
in die weite Welt hinein . . ."

So there we sit in the grautestov, ja,
my Haenschen in his fancy shoes
and his Haenschen in bluejeans
and the girls with Englische names even.
Who would say we Mennonitisch are?

How we think, even,
is all aufgemixed.
Big Haenschen has his head all full of Reform,
and little Haenschen preaches the N.D.P.,
but you can still see it,
it's the same, how they walk,
the real Mennonite way,
like bringing in the cows . . .
except maybe too much sometimes
what was once on the boots clinging
now from the tongue falls, ja?

TANTE TINA REFLECTS ON MAGGIE THATCHER

for Jim Reimer

That woman, ach du lieber,
no sauce on her verenicke
she's got, that's what, too much
pasty dough and two-per-cent milk.
She should come to sengerfest
and sing along with all the other old ladies.
"O that I had a thousand tongues"
she should like, ja?
not all this stuff of never giving in.
She gave in long ago.
To rest by Ronald Reagan on his horse
her mind was laid.
Kids, even, they have, runt weanlings with diaper pins
in their ears, a hopeless bunch,
rock throwers, pinches off the old dough ball herself,
left too long in the oven,
like geroestete zwieback.

Maggie herself,
she too is geroestet.
She needs dipping in some tea,
get those buns wet already yet,
a good immersion baptism, and then
confession: Lieben sie die Brueder?
Let her confess before the whole church
how she found the Lord
right here at Tina's place.
Let her confess how Tina sat her down
with paska and glums, Tina ladled
all that pluma moos out of her head,

gave her potatoes to think about,
where they come from, and eggs,
let her shovel some of that other stuff
the chickens make,
she makes so well herself,
gave her halvah just to keep the plumbing clear.
Let her confess how Tina made verenicke
and Jim Reimer himself made the sauce
so good the Lord would eat.

Ach, Mrs. Thatcher, come down to Altona.
Change your name: Magdalena Thiessen
is much nicer, ja?
Flop your buns down in the kitchen here.
Confess a little. It's good for the bunyans.
So bad the world can't be
there's no hope.
You just come down here to Tina's.
We'll get you back in shape.
Then we can do something
about those men.

TANTE TINA CALLS IN TO A RADIO TALK SHOW

Hello? Is this the radio?
The talk-in show? Ja, it's me,
Tina, again. Like a pig this thing squeals.
Turn my radio down? Ja. Just a minute. O.K.

Ja, now I think the Russian
invasion of Grenada – pardon?
ja, I mean the American invasion
on Afghanistan – no, ja,
you know what I mean,
like the British when they came to Manitoba
when Louis Riel was here.
That's when the Harry Dick family
from our village in Russia came
but then they went to Mexico, because here it was all
so Englisch, you know?
But now his children
are coming back. Better knacksaut here
I say, ha ha. Ja. Altona is the sunflower
capital of Canada. Harry Dick,
he was my mother's uncle.
Tante Kate, she stayed here.
Twelve children, she told Uncle Fritz,
I'm not dragging them to Fernheim
just so we can have no rubber tires.
But some, like the Peter Dicks,
they went too and liked it.
No, I don't think they went to Grenada.
But Harry Peters, when he left Russia,
he came through Afghanistan,
and his children are now missionaries in India.

Ja, O.K., I'll be short.
What my idea is,
I think they should all come back
to Manitoba – pardon?
Ja, I don't care, the Russians, the Americans, the Harry Dicks,
whoever. My Tante Frieda, she's still in Russia,
at Alma Ata, and Lydia Franz's boy, Fred,
he lives in America, in Fresno.
So you see?

O.K., I have to go now.
The platz is burning.

CANADIAN BABEL

Jake Peters returns to Canada after twenty years on the mission field in India and calls "Cross Canada Checkup" to give his solution to the Canadian Crisis

Hello? Is this the CBC?
Ja, it's me, Jake Peters from Altona.
In Manitoba. The sunflower capital, ja,
so you know already.
I am already a solution having
for all this constitutional problems yet.
It's too many immigrants.

Ja, I think we should all the Englische people
be sending home who are speaking funny
so we can't understand.
Then we can the country be starting over.
The Chinese first, they are from Hong Kong coming
thinking they can anything buy here
my Truda tells me from Vancouver.
Even the government they are thinking they can buy.
Well maybe it's so, ja?
Mr. Mulroney, he is Irish
and they are fighting always and drinking
so they for sure should be home going
with their music fiddling on the TV also.
The Indians, too, the real ones from India,
they are here coming
and so hard working they can buy the Thiessens'
farm in Coaldale, ja, George Thiessen whose father
was killed by the Bolsheviks,
how can that right be?
And the other Indians, the lazy ones

who are sugar beets picking
and beer drinking
they can be back going to the bush.
And the Ukrainians they are having their own place now
where they can go. It's not necessary for them
here to be complaining about the kommunists.

Even from Quebec the French-speaking Englische
are coming here so I can't versteh
at DeFehr's Supermarket in Winkler even.
They are building monuments and stadiums
that are down falling, like Stalin's, ja,
not like Dueck's Construction in Plum Coulee,
so I think they should home be going also
to France. We don't need such monuments here.
And the British, they are speaking funny
like the queen, and they are having their noses in the air
like they have been behind the barn walking.

Ja? Ja, they should all go home
now, all the Englische,
What do you say? the Mennonites?
Ja, well maybe the non-churchly ones,
the ones who are off gefallen,
they can again to Russia be going,
but me, after doing the Lord's work
with the heathen so many years
and all the churchly Mennonites,
we should here be staying,
this is our promised land, ja.

Where is there else to be going?

A REQUEST FROM TANTE TINA TO THE MENNONITE WOMEN'S MISSIONARY SOCIETY TO PUT SALMAN RUSHDIE ON THE PRAYER LIST

Dear sisters in the Lord.
Sometimes when I am the chickens feeding
and the radio by the barn plays,
even like a mother hen the Lord
is me to the kernels of His wisdom guiding.
Many times has the Lord reminded me from
the days in Russia. When the Indians
in Quebec have their guns taken
their graveyard to defend
against a golf course,
I have remembered the Bolsheviks
and how they came to our village
and a factory from the church made.
Ja, but this morning this is not
what I am wanting to say to you.

I have on the radio heard
how the Ayatollah in Iran is wanting
to kill this Salman Rushdie
because he is telling stories
that the Ayatollah doesn't like.
I am thinking then about how John Friesen
has once a letter in Russia written
during the time of Stalin,
and after, how they took him away
just as he the Bible was reading
at the supper table,
and his wife Elsie and the five children
have him never seen again.

Elsie has told me that John the parable
of Jesus was reading about the vineyard
rented to the workers who all the servants
of the owner killed, even the very son,
and then John told how we the earth are renting
from God, and when He comes to ask,
well, how goes it,
what can we say?
And then the kommunists have come
and John has been taken away
and then they have prayed
and then they have schnetki eaten.

And I have told Elsie
that God is in that story,
and how much Jesus is stories loving,
ja, the truth comes to us that way
and we can eat schnetki and life is going on
even then, ja? That is why Stalin and the Ayatollah
and even some Christians
do not like stories so much
because they think maybe God
is in the story hiding like meat in a fleisch piroshki,
and when we open the bun
God is on us checking to ask
how we are caring for the beautiful vineyard.

This they do not like,
that maybe God is looking,
and that is why I am asking the church
to put Mr. Rushdie on the missionary prayer list.
As the grain from the leaky pail to the chickens
falls, so can God through Mr. Rushdie
into the world be coming.

And if we the leaky pails are making silent,
then who among us will the Lord's voice be?
Will not even the corn cry out?
Ja.
So, let us pray.

TANTE TINA RETURNS FROM VISITING HER COUSIN IN MEXICO AND GOES TO THE GROCERY STORE WITH HER GRANDSON LITTLE HAENSCHEN

for Graeme Gibson

When I have just from Mexico
been coming back,
from visiting Elfrieda,
I have gone with my grandboy Haenschen
to Thiessen's Grocery Market
and there by the tomatoes
I have the sign
from Mexico seen.

Haenschen, I have said,
if these are from Mexico coming
what are they in Altona doing?
Have we no tomatoes here?
What is Peter Enns on his place making now?
Ja, Oma, he said, we have tomatoes,
but these are cheaper.
Peter Enns, he is in the city now working
for Toews Furniture.
This is now free trade
which will make us all have more money.
And I can see the grandboy is watching me
from the side to see what I will be saying.

And then for no reason
I have by the tomatoes
shouted until my voice is broken:
I have seen in Mexico

they are having no bathrooms
so they in the field have to go,
even on the tomatoes they are going,
and the children are in rags
and have only old tomatoes to eat.
And Peter Enns, is he in the city
because this is what he is wanting?
What is being cheaper?
Who has decided these things?

And they have taken me away then
from the store and put into the car,
and little Haenschen has the groceries to get
by himself. By myself
I am thinking about Stalin,
how he everything in one big
company was wanting to make,
and to be deciding our lives
from Moscow.
And now the Wall is coming down
and Stalin is winning, only he is calling
himself something else.
Big Haenschen says it is not Stalin.
The food is from Kraft coming,
and General Foods, and they are in America
where there is no Stalin.

But I am knowing better, ja?
And now I am also too old,
so I can see there is nothing new under the sun,
everything is the same,
and the real menschen are always put last,
and my own boy is putting me into the home.
But the grandboy, he knows.

He is wanting to take me again
to Thiessen's grocery.
He is wondering if this time we can
about the green peppers talk.

TANTE TINA REMEMBERS TRUDEAU

for Maggie D., at her 50th birthday

Everyone is today Trudeau forgetting
or bad things about him saying,
but I think he should come down to my place
in Altona. I will make him some borscht,
and rollkuchen with honey
from the Thiessen place in Beaver Lodge.

And we can talk.
I will even some French for him be trying,
and maybe he can speak some Low German.
More tongues we need in this place,
not fewer. My man Doft has told me once
I am Mr. Trudeau loving too much and
he thinks I would like to kiss him,
or to run away with him even.
Well, maybe it's true
and I am sad
because there are no more politicians
I am feeling like kissing.
He the last one was, ja?
When we first came to this country
the Liberals were letting us in.
And when I am old,
Mr. Trudeau has me a cheque given
for old age pension. No one has such a thing
heard before in Coaldale or Altona.

Now all the lazy people want only
to speak in one tongue
like before Babel, but the Lord knows

this is only for money-making good.
For the borscht, the more things go in
the better the eating.
Ah, ja, what do I know,
but when the Holy Spirit came
and everyone was in tongues speaking
they did not all babble the same,
they only understood each other.
Already each tongue
their own country wants,
like Manning and Parizeau, but they are small
people, with visions like a rooster.
For myself, I would rather into the new year
porzeltche with Trudeau be eating
than mannagruetze with Manning.

But no one listens to an old lady
anymore, ja? So when we each
are sitting alone, speaking to ourselves
in our own tongue, like Mr. Toews here in the home
who always into his soup mumbles,
maybe they will remember me,
and Mr. Trudeau even,
and they will see, even if a man sometimes
wrong is, it is good to have someone
around to be giving a kiss, ja?

TANTE TINA PUTS THE GULF WAR INTO PERSPECTIVE

for my mother

I have a right to be cranky, ja.
I am an old lady.
But I'm not gone yet.
You come sitz mal here,
Na, a little closer.
I already have to talk so loud
my hearing goes.
But I think still, ja?

One time when I was little still in Russia
in the war, before the unsettling to Canada,
I was maybe five maybe six years old, you listen mal
you're not so busy,
a man to the door was pummelling
at night, his hand bleeding in a torn shirt.
He was dirty, I could smell even,
not like the barn smelling, not like pigs
in spring, like old meat more, wurst gone bad.
His eyes were deep like the broken well with no water.
Mutti took him in, and has made him soup –
kertofel and hot water, it was all.
I was by the stove scared while he is slurping.
And then Mutti him to the bed showed
where Uncle Peter slept before they took him
and Papa. I was so tight holding
to Mutti's rough wool my fingers were aching.

We were just to bed going then,
the candle auss-poosting, and more men came,

krass, loud, shouting even more than you
and Papa sometimes. They grabbed the man from the bed,
his feet banging on the floor,
and outside by the barn there was a crash.

The men left and we sat on the bed,
still, Mutti squeezing my hand
and then letting go and then squeezing again.
Finally with one hand she takes me
and a pail with water in the other
like she knows what she must do.

Come, Tina, she says, and we walk through the dark
where the cows were – we have them all
eaten, and Fritz the dog also – and there outside
by the door is the man, like a sack.
He is again with dirt and blood besmeared
so Mutti takes the water and I too
and we wash him. This could be Papa, she says.
This could somewhere be your Papa.
Always she looks over her shoulder.
I am thinking maybe the men will come back
but I am not afraid. Mutti and I are washing
a man who could be like Papa who went away.

His face I can't remember
so I look very close at the dead man's face.
I wonder is he a Kommunist or a Machnovski
or for the Czar or maybe just like Papa.
Now anyway he is just a dead man.
Mutti puts him in Papa's clean white shirt
and upsits him by the wall and we pray:
Lieber Gott what we can
we have done. Now You do.

After, I sleep with Mutti under the blue quilt.
I wonder if the dead man is cold outside.

Why am I telling you this? Just listen mal
to an old lady for once. In the morning
I through the shed run to the outside
and the man is gone.
I know God has done something
and I am glad, because maybe he was Papa.

All my life I carry that inside.
Never I told you. Maybe even I just remember it now.
But today I see on TV here Mr. Bursch
the president. Ja, I know who I mean,
don't interrupt. Mr. Bursch and Mr. Saddam and Mr. Shamir
and Schwartzkopf and Yasser, the whole pack of them
they make widows and blame God, ja?
They want to look strong, because they are cowards.
They are killing men like Papa.
Ja, I know there are reasons,
always there are reasons to kill, ja?
Always the same.

I am thinking some Mutti
is missing her Papa, and some little Tina somewhere.
Maybe he is dead in the road
or by a shed in the sand. She doesn't know.
And little Tina is afraid but she must clean the body
so God can come and do something.

You have a meeting, I know,
but I have seen the pictures on TV
and I am remembering. I must tell someone.
And if not my Haenschen then who?

Sometimes you young people see only pictures, ja?
You don't know. Sometimes I think a good thing
would be if there were bombs in Washington or Ottawa,
then maybe those men would not be so krass.
You go now to your meeting.
Maybe another time when you come
the Lord will already have taken me.

Say hello to little Haenschen.
Tell him to come sometimes again guitar playing.
The time then is not so long.
Now go once. I have to sleep.

SINGING OUR SOULS INTO LIGHT

BIRD OF PREY

Turning high above the clefts and hillocks
in the clear silence
in the cool silken blue sweep of sky,
a sharp, anxious fear comes piercing like a sudden cry:
is it my turn to be home feeding the nestlings?
have I left the oven on?
does some hunter have her sights on me?
is this merely my stupid fear of heights?
am I a white male?
was my first language German?
is this all my fault?
when I arrive home, will the nest be empty?

The land shimmers and lifts.
A small brown mouse quivers in a furry cleft.
The thoughtless plunge engulfs me,
down through darkness
the bright bottomless thrill
the wriggling flash of life, the quick throb
here in my talons.
Gotcha!

The wild furry thing is mine.
I squeeze and squeeze
until my fears are still
until the thing is still

and I am lifting, giddy, full of light.
The clefts and hillocks fall away from me
so far away. I am again the cool dark point,

the heavens turning slowly at my wingtips.
From my claw-tip drops the frail, wet-feathered nestling.

The arrow spears again, cupid's shadow,
the hunter with her finger on the bow
of my regrets for what I've done, have not done,
have undone, cannot remember,
have not conceived.
The perfect two-kid two-car TV CD green lawn predator
I once despised
I have become.
I have no right to be here.
This is no one's sky.

There is no place to be
but here.
This is the story of my life.

THE SHIPS AT SANTA CRUZ

for Jim, at his 60th, with a wish for many more sailing days

Like fins of great white sharks
the ships at Santa Cruz
cruise the horizon, the future
out there, too many choppy miles away
to fret about.

The kids and I are building sand castles
on the beach. This is all in the present:
sand hot-dry, cold-wet, sun-singed skin, the fortress
complete with moat and digging beetles
pried out of a hole by Matthew's nimble tines.

A freak wave from the incoming tide
catapults against the castle's west wall
which hesitates, uncertainly,
before sagging.

I lift my eyes to the ships.
More like white sheets on the line, I'd say,
today laundered by tomorrow's
slippery thinking.
Matthew and Rebecca are burying themselves
in the sand, laughing as the sea
licks at them with its playful come-ons.
They don't imagine as far as the horizon.
These few watery, arctic fingers
are diversion enough.

Up the beach, firm-bodied throw-backs
play volleyball, not so much for the game

as for this moment, the clear, non-thinking
sun-blessed sense of self.
Nobody else seems to be heeding those white things –
sharks, sheets, whatever. I see now
I'll have to worry out these matters
for everyone on the beach.

There is some logic in this, in getting sand
up your crotch, risking cancer for a good broil,
rescuing a pigeon from the kelp-litter,
exploring caves, lazing over champagne
and eggs sardu for breakfast, or even just
being here.
There is no space for mid-life crises
in a life lived daily. And the longer mid-life gets
put off, the longer life, not so?

The past is an uninhabitable planet
(don't dwell on it, we're counselled).
I've been there, anyway.
The future? The ships' sails
are bleached, white flags,
flapping in the bright sun,
promise of a truce
in these constant battles.

At the evening wiener roast,
sun laid back in languorous hues
against the soft dusk, a young mother
stands at sea's edge, babe in arms,
nine-year-old Rebecca at her side.
When the sea makes its expected
unexpected plunge, Rebecca like a sand-sprite
skips away. The mother slips,

holding up her baby, freedom's torch.
She laughs, wet-bottomed, knowing suddenly
what she once knew, should have known . . .

expect life to startle you,
and when it does, laugh, or drown.
The baby, wide-eyed that anything
out there could be so starkly cold,
chuckles at a warm teat.

We huddle around our fire
singing summer songs:
"Rolling along the open road."
The horizon is so deeply dark
that sea and sky are one.
The ships at Santa Cruz slip
sleekly into the lagoon.
I see now that they are just ships
after all, with people on them,
braced with sea winds and salt
and tales of almost caught
glints from the deep,

making plans for another day of sailing.

JUST ANOTHER EXCUSE FOR A CAT

for TNT and the family pets

There is one room
in your heart
where only
a friend can come.
He checks the closet
for old hangers. He cares
about what the stain
on the floor says
about you.

When your friend
leaves, you think
about a dog.
A dog will check your closet
if you check the closet.
He will look at the stain
if you look at the stain.
He will lie down
on the floor
thinking
about food.

You are thinking
maybe a pocket pet
would do. A hamster or a gerbil
will propel its plastic sphere
anywhere –
over the floor
into the closet.
The friends' room

will be the limits
of its world.
It will have no perspective
on the carpet stain.
It will pause
when it hears you leave,
thinking
about cats.

A cat is an island
you can visit
in your room.
He will not care
about the hangers
or the floor.
He will give you a warm body
sometimes, when he is not preoccupied
with squirrels.
He will not know
what this means to you.

When your friend
leaves, there will be
a scratching at the corner
of your heart.
You will sit in your room
with your hand kneading
the cat.
The cat will hear the scratch.
He will put one ear forward
and one backward, thinking
about dogs and gerbils.

You will feel the scratch.
You will think
about your friend.
You will be fingering the cat's
vibrating fur.
After a while, you will forget
what it was
you were thinking.

Then you can both return to work
scrubbing at the carpet stain,
and studying squirrel behaviour
in an apple tree.

WHY YOU ARE SMILING AT BREAKFAST

for Andreas Schroeder

When you haven't seen a friend
for a good long time –
you were busy, or distant –
you are not even thinking about him
while you stare at the chickadees
flitting from the feedbox.
At dusk a cardinal
impiously bright
alights at the window.

Lace curtains of wet snowflakes fall
like unresolved
memories, like softly falling birds
dying across night's darkening mind.

Just when you think you are asleep
the friend appears, stomping his shoes on the doormat.
He throws his arms around you
and hugs. The darkness crackles
from your ribs.

There is no reason for this.
No preparation.
No time for questions. He is off,
gritty snow left puddling on the kitchen floor.

You are left, falling lightly in a field of snow,
smiling at the ceiling.

By breakfast, sleep has mopped the heart's linoleum.
You do not understand why you are humming
as you pour the coffee.

SASKATOON REVISITED

for ABR on her 19th birthday

I'd forgotten how it feels
to lie back against the dry prickles
of grass, how the sky splits open above me
infinitely blue, breathless, and the bottom
drops out, how I fall, freely, chuteless,
floating into the hissing, high-winged silence.
And far below, a red convertible
and thoughtless couples on the grass
with ice cream; and all along the river's aisles,
where Frisbees hum like empty offering plates
across the stinging sands,
pace slow canoes.

The city is surrounded
by its clouds of witnesses, the heroes,
farmers, the stubborn ones, saints,
the poor, red-eyed ones,
lines of dust like clefts of unsung hymns
ruled across their brows.
The wind is preaching again.
Failed crops! it cries. No rain!
The dust wags a stern finger
across the fields. Let this be a lesson:

organize
conserve
buy insurance.

Move to Toronto.

But here, in the bright centre of this moment,
there is only the startling, bottomless blue,
the giddy thrill of flying
and a spirit suddenly, sunfully innocent,
my head thrown back as I lay a fuming streak of rubber
across the prairie skyway
singing

like a choir of crazy locusts.

ONE OF THOSE FLIGHT DREAMS

I paddle in the swirling pools
at Keiteur Falls' edge, taunting:
come current, free me.
Just feet away the cliff drops, stunning, mystical.
Like eddies at the precipice
my thoughts tease, prying loose
those other lives I left, promising the thrill
of the great, heart-rending plunge

into the mist. We play with dreams
of flight, then walk. Our dreams come down
to airplane fantasies, capsules that propel us, there to here.
And back.

I am recalling how, at the lip of the escarpment,
I slipped and clung, wet and laughing

to the rocks.

Georgetown, Guyana

THE SNOW FORT

Once a year we built a fort –
Matthew, Rebecca, and I –
from hardened snow, till our cheeks hurt
from the bite of the wintry blue sky.

Once a year we stacked the chunks
of uneven, prickly ice
till, walls over eyeballs, out of the wind,
we vanished without a trace.

Only our bodies, once a year,
kept up the appearance of us,
while we clambered misty snowbound peaks
and hummed Amazing Grace.

We only came back if the sky fell down
and bonked us on the head
or someone was calling Dinner Time!
or our toes felt like cold lead.

Yes, once a year we built that place –
Matthew, Rebecca, and I –
cheek by toe, on fire, in ice,
biting back at the wintry blue sky.

FOR ONE BLESSED MOMENT

for Dale Mieske, actor, friend – teacher – for many blessed moments

When all the sheep are numbered
and all the lambs, the lame,
the wet-bummed stragglers,
the little stiff ones,
are computerized, counted, abstracted
into "y" as a function of "x,"

when most of the wallpaper
some of the wall
and all my weekend home-fixer spirits
have come down,

when my back gets thrown out
with the trash,

I remember the man on the stage,
how the make-up kisses his face
how he slips on his costume
how he teaches me the art of making up
after my quarrels with the world,
slips on a peel of laughter
with grace,
his voice like a bright macaw
trailing red and white and black ribbons from his mouth
fluttering into my face
where the little claws cling
to the bone of my nose,
how the play slips like a kid glove
softly over my wounds.

When all my days are numbered,
the lame, the stiff ones added up,
results from life's double-blind trial
about to be tabulated, abstracted,
and why why why
prepares to meet its equal,

that moment, a kitten, restrained,
tight-sprung on my kid-gloved palm,
will once more speak,
and in that darkness I shall laugh
to feel the ribbons brush my cheek.

THE CARAPHIN POEM

a poem to celebrate the Caribbean Animal and Plant Health Information Network, Trinidad, July 12, 1991

We are all islands,
you and I. Singing coral,
we are delicate and sharp,
decked in black spiny urchins,
with beautiful stag-horned backup,
our brain flowers blossoming.
We sing alone
in the pan-dancing night.

Though we be islands,
we celebrate not shores, but
what we sling between us,
the beauty of our nets,
how we get buoyed up,
how we leap from coral fires
into the sizzling steel-drummed dance.

We celebrate the tugs from deep down,
the ones that nip and slip away,
barracuda, rosy damselfish,
rock beauties, hawkfish, sharks,
the angels of shadow,
the ones that get you in just the right muscle,
the heart, with their jazzy style:
the slim-bodied trumpets,
saucer-eyed porgy,
grunts and parrots, sand drums,
reef croaker, and the sweet-talking
peppermint bass.

This dance we live has plenty
to set the gills a-tingle.
to make the islands bloom,
tree, branch and leaf coral,
food in the belly,
and we, this paradox,
all islands, jumping up
together, fish skipping over wave-tips
in the pan-dancing night.

THE SHADOW

for Di Brandt, who articulated questions we were not supposed to ask, and set them free

loping over the moon-white ice, my soles barely skimming the
stinging crust. slim, mottled, luminescent trees around me,
supplicating the moon's hem. i thrill unthinking, in free sheer
flight across the back night.

in mid-stride, in the corner of my eye

a shadow flits out of the cold-crackling trees. a lean, loping
fear, it leaps

This is when Kathy heard me whimpering and woke me up, I
explain at the breakfast table, and Matthew, at six years before
the very gates to the kingdom, asks

were you the wolf, Daddy?

A MOMENT IN TIME

> "If you do not know how to die, never trouble yourself; Nature will in a moment fully and sufficiently instruct you; she will exactly do that business for you, take you no care for it."
>
> – Montaigne

Through a room of nineteenth century
marbles, two lofty rows of solid bodies,
poised like a gauntlet of choices
in the monumental cool stillness,
I walk, pondering:
which would I prefer,
the sudden oblivion of a collision,
the lingering death of a body
reclaimed by nature, cell by cell,
or this, like Lot's wife,
forever held in one pure, timeless moment?
And if I could choose,
which moment? What is my final pose
without repose?
The sensuous hauteur of a young girl,
the wistful, armladen mother,
the rebellious man bent over, hands wrenched
against ropes at his back,
the heroic warrior, blade raised, cocky as crabgrass?
All are equally well-muscled, smooth
to touch, forever strong.

Pick your moment, your pose,
then look, there's Gomorrah
and for you, no tomorrow.
I pause, indecisive in this vault
of distilled discomfited time.

I see people in mid-stride, mid-struggle, mid-sentence,
pushing against the stone, eager for life
too soon in death. They await a whistle,
a kiss, or at least more visitors:
they couldn't let all hell break loose
with just me here. An audience is called for,
fleeing in screams
from the miraculous, bursting stone.

Some day all hell will break loose,
a meteoric collision maybe, or more likely
a frustrated general, or, most likely,
just more of the same old acid rain, nucleotech,
biotech, technofix, the chronic exhaust of progress
into oblivion.

These smug statues will still be here
gathering dust, with me perhaps among them,
unable to decide
which pose is exactly right,
caught one day, off guard,
stealing candy from my daughter's Hallowe'en bag.

at the Ny Carlsberg Glyptotek, Copenhagen

FORTY LIES (AND SOME TRUTH) FOR MY FORTIETH BIRTHDAY

Trust me,
the truth lies
somewhere in between.

At the end of time, your ship lies
at anchor. In the beginning,
two people lie down together. Time flies
when you're having a good time.

I don't feel
a day older. I'm not getting older,
I'm getting wiser. At least I'm wise
to that one.

How you lie – the curves of your body's form
in the grass, how the wind's lips
touch you – is important. And how you rise
to whatever occasion. Farewells for instance.
I could never say goodbye the proper way, just the right
combination of tears and cheerful lies.
Just snip! and time is cut.
I am free, falling into an abyss.
I am soaring over the Lethbridge Coulee.
Life goes on just the same, only more.

The apple tree outside my window is old
and still bursting with flowers. In fall, the rank
sweetness of fallen apples gives me hope.
The kids can pick up the apples, two cents each,
and put them into the compost.
I check my wallet and hope there aren't as many

as it looks. When the kids come in
with apple-red cheeks they don't ask for money.
I am nauseous with optimism.

At mid-life, in the middle of a poem,
I wonder what's left to say.
The first forty years are full of answers.
The answer lies all around you.
The answer lies in your heart.
Love is the answer. Marigolds, permanent revolution,
Lucy and Gorbachev.

After forty, the answers are questionable.

What is love? Who is Gorbachev?
Does anyone remember Dubček?

I remember a bottle of white wine, a bubble bath,
our bodies like soap, diligently cleansing
our soiled oracles. I see a rolling, treed graveyard
with turtles and frogs plopping
and black flies at my bum.
We are debating potash cartels,
how the moral refinements of uranium spokesmen
can kill you, how Abbie Hoffman knew
about the real Kissinger, and what
we should do with ourselves now that we are
over thirty and too old to be trusted.

I remember the Czech in the Madras hostel,
a little irrepressible professor from Brno:
The Russians will never invade! he gushed.
Still, the kids did pick up the apples.
And there is Gorbachev.

Forty is just another birthday.
There is no connection
between what I remember was
and what I hoped might be.

At the birthday party I spilled champagne
on my lap, a symbolic toast
to my lost youth. The memory spills over me
like orange juice, sweet, sticky,
leaving an embarrassing stain.
I am nostalgic.
I am surprised. All these over-forties around me
at the table – we look so young.
We hug each other and kiss.

The kids are sleeping upstairs.
They are still so young, too young to understand this:
all these deep emotions
like a fruit stew. I'll feel full for years.
I deserve this.

I've made my bed
and now I have to lie in it.
The future lies before me.

NATURAL LOVE

for K.

There is no love in clouds,
for though I cycle with the best morale
they time their heed to nature's call
just when I take the road.

There is no love in soil,
the righteous sweat I pour into the compost hole
upheaved, discarded by raccoons
who from my spare cuisine recoil.

There is no love in air,
for though I use no aerosol
winter abuses with an icy claw,
and summer spites me with an ozone stare.

There is no love in cats;
although I feed them low-ash friendly
crunch, and fondle them, they bring me fleas,
and flopping birds, though, thankfully, not rats.

And even the tomatoes, fed
and watered with a loving hand, respond
with bugs and fungus and,
at harvest time, with being soft, and dead.

Oh love, come read me now,
for nowhere is love writ but where your tongue
inscribes, and nowhere read but where your lingering
fingers tread the braille, and all that nature knows

is scripted by the tussle
of our bodies' calligraphic brush.

CORPOREAL LOVE

I love the body
earth's body
the body of Christ
your body.
Your mind is nothing without your body.
The spirit of earth is nothing without
the trees, mud, cats, snakes,
children, grandparents.
Victory in war is nothing
without bodies to count.
Bodies count.

I love bodies.
I want to kiss them, hold them, pity them,
refrain from embracing even
as I embrace.
I want to speak unspeakable emotions
in body language.

Whatever we cannot say
we are fated to embody.
Whatever we mean
is meant best with our bodies.
These are the words of God,
incarnation, beyond creeds
and commanding textbooks,
infinity embracing herself,
loving ourselves to life
even unto death.

And what I wish for everyone,
my global fatherhood peace wish,
comes down to a bowl of chili
and buttered toast,
with English Breakfast tea,
with you, in this warm kitchen
on a snow-blown day.

THE EDITOR'S SONG

for Marg Reimer

i.

The editor opens her door
to the waggish introit of words,
cute, nervous playthings with teeth,
the comfort of children.

To welcome words is an act of faith,
to utter them again, of hope.

One day, a rabid Pekinese is at her door,
or a treacherous pack of Spaniels
baring teeth in pain or anger,
or dragging broken limbs, whimpering.
The nature of these visits is unpredictable,
deceptive as the hunting Poodles
we train to dance and make us laugh.
We work our warp into their woof
then claim it as the Word:
this is true Nature, this the Truth.
But even as we speak
the Heeler slinks up from behind
to sink her teeth into our tendons,
proclaiming with a low growl:
is this then your intention?

ii.

Let us sing now a hymn to the healer,
physician of the broken tongue,
judge of the merciful sentence.
She puts to rest the phobic snarl
and casts the fractured prose
in plastered splints.
She returns the verb to its subject,
the subject to its rightful heir.

Let us sing the waggish words,
the healed ones,
the friendly ones, by firesides
and bounding near on long walks,
snuffling playfully in dark rock-fissures
and thorny shrubs.

Let us sing also between the lines,
the harmony of spaces,
the resonance of what is left unsaid;
sing the witless howl, on leash,
unleashed.

iii.

Let us sing to the Healer
who gathers our voice in the night
and returns it again on the Wind.
In the singing, in the returning song,
we can almost believe we are more
than we are, can almost believe
in our beauty.

At the edge of the clearing
at the edge of the forest primeval
at the verge of believing
at the cliff of becoming
on the wind, turning,
our howl is returning, the round song
the word, spurning void.

In the night of our singing
the light we are given, have given,
is gathered, is given once more
in the round perfect moon of our singing.
In the pale of our night
by the wit of our tone
by the translucent bone in the teeth of our tongue

we are singing our souls into Light.

"Breaking Free the Whales": In 1988, an international mission was organized to rescue several whales separated from their pod and trapped in the arctic ice off Alaska. The action was massive, expensive, and probably, ultimately, detrimental to the wild population of whales, and made a great many people feel good about themselves. It was typical, in other words, not only of how we usually show our affection for nature, but for each other.

"A Word in the Nest": *Forever Summer, Forever Sunday Peter Gerhard Rempel's Photographs of Mennonites in Russia, 1890-1917*, with introduction and editing by John D. Rempel and Paul Tiessen, was published by Sand Hill Books, Inc., St. Jacobs, Ontario, 1981.

Mennonite Blues: A number of these poems draw, for both words and syntax, on High German (which the Mennonite community I grew up in used for education and religion – that is, high culture), and Low German, which is rooted in an oral, rather than a written, tradition. Low German (plautdietsch, or, literally, Flat German), comes originally from the flat lands of Northern Germany and the Netherlands, and was carried along as a functional "mother tongue" as Mennonites migrated across Europe, into the Russian Empire, and finally around the world. It was a language used on the farm, for down-to-earth real-life conversations, and which my parents used to keep secrets from us children. Thus, while I picked up the rhythm of the tongue, I cannot myself speak it.

If you want to find out more about this stuff, track down a Mennonite whose ancestors migrated over from the Ukraine sometime in the last century – people with names like Friesen, Reimer, Rempel, Toews, and Thiessen. There are a lot of them in southern Manitoba. I'd send you to books, of which there are a few, but this is one case where books can never do the language justice. You really need to talk to someone. The same holds true for the songs used in the poems. You can see some of them in Mennonite hymnals, but you'll be better off (and no doubt a better person) hearing them sung in four-part harmony. Visit a local Mennonite Church; check ahead to make sure they're the singing kind (some of them aren't). There's really no substitute for the real thing.

Where an umlaut would be used in the German, I have put an *e* after the letter, both to help non-German readers with pronunciation, and to foster the process of having these words incorporated into the English language.

I have not italicized any of the German or Low German words. A sign of the great vitality and health of the English language – of any language – is its ability to embrace words from many different linguistic sources. The germanic words in these poems are my small contribution to the future health of English.

"The CARAPHIN Poem": Pan is the traditional music of Trinidad and Tobago, played with mallets on hand-made steel drums. If your body doesn't move when this music plays, you're either a Mennonite, or you're in trouble. If your body moves, and you are a Mennonite, then you really are in trouble.

ACKNOWLEDGEMENTS

COLLECTIONS

Nine of these poems (all from the "Mennonite Blues" section) have been previously collected in *Good Housekeeping* (1983) and *Endangered Species* (1988)

Many of the poems in this collection have appeared previously in the following:

ANTHOLOGIES

Acts of Concealment: Mennonite/s Writing in Canada; *A Sense of Place*; *Three Mennonite Poets.*

MAGAZINES AND JOURNALS

Canadian Forum; *The Fiddlehead*; *Grain*; *Negative Capability*; *The New Quarterly*; *Prairie Fire*; *Worldscape.*

OTHER

"Just Another Excuse for a Cat" was displayed in large poster format at an international conference on human-animal interactions, "Animals & Us," in Montreal, 1992.

"A Request from Tante Tina" was performed, in costume, at the Twentieth Anniversary Banquet of the Writers' Union of Canada, Ottawa, 1993.

Several of the poems appeared as chapter breaks in my non-fiction book *Food, Sex & Salmonella: The Risks of Environmental Intimacy*

Special thanks to Stan Dragland for his helpful editorial advice.